EXPLORERS CLUB

AVALANCHE *in the* ALPS

by Betsy Loredo

Illustrated by
Michael Moran

SILVER MOON PRESS
NEW YORK

This book was created in cooperation with the National Oceanic and Atmospheric Administration, Washington D.C. The publisher would also like to thank Professor Christopher Exline of the University of Nevada — Reno for his help in preparing this book.

For information contact:
Silver Moon Press, 126 Fifth Avenue, Suite 803,
New York, New York 10011

Designed by Geoffrey Notkin
Cover Illustration by Michael Moran

Printed in the United States of America

Library of Congress Cataloging-in-Publication Data

Loredo, Betsy, 1963-
    Avalanche in the Alps/by Betsy Loredo; illustrated by Michael Moran – 1st ed.
    p. cm. – (The Explorers Club)
    "Created in cooperation with the National Oceanic and Atmospheric Administration, Washington, D.C." – T.p. verso
    Summary: In Switzerland for a vacation in the Alps, members of the Explorers Club encounter spectacular views, serious hiking trails, and an avalanche.
    ISBN 1-881889-12-2: $12.95
    [1. Alps – Fiction. 2. Switzerland – Fiction. 3. Explorers – Fiction. 4. Travel – Fiction. 5. Clubs – Fiction.] I. Moran, Michael, 1957- ill. II. United States. National Oceanic and Atmospheric Administration. III. Title. IV. Series: Loredo, Betsy, 1963- Explorers Club.
    PZ7.L8786Av 1993
    [Fic] – dc20   93-11175
                                                        CIP
                                                        AC

CHAPTER ONE

"We're going *where*?" Amy Buckley gasped.

The Buckley family was sitting at their kitchen table one Friday evening when Mr. Buckley made his announcement.

"We're going to Switzerland," he repeated.

Amy was so excited she almost spilled a bowl of peas right into her brother's lap.

"Hey, watch it!" Larry yelped, when the vegetables tilted in his direction.

"Sorry," Amy said to her brother, "but didn't you hear?"

"I heard," Larry said. He turned to his father. "Why Switzerland, Dad? What are you working on this time?"

Mr. Buckley was an engineer. His building projects

sometimes took the family to far-off places.

"Is it a bridge?" Amy guessed. "Or a tunnel?"

"This time it's something a little different," Mr. Buckley explained. "I have to go to the Alps to check up on a special ski lift system I helped design a few years ago."

"A ski lift?" Amy said. "I guess that means the Alps is a mountain."

"It's a whole lot of mountains," Larry said. "You'd know that if you did your homework," he added smugly.

"I do my homework. We just haven't gotten to the Alps yet. I can't help it if you're two grades ahead of me," Amy replied.

Amy was 11, two years younger than Larry. Amy had inherited their father's red hair, sky-blue eyes and freckles; Larry looked more like their mother, with his shaggy brown hair and darker blue eyes. Sometimes Amy thought the only thing she and Larry had in common was their fiery temper.

"Come on, you two," Mrs. Buckley said. "This is good news, remember?"

"It sure is," Amy said. "I bet there'll be snow."

"It's April already. It's too warm for snow," Larry said.

"It's warm here in Maryland, but it'll be cold in the mountains." Amy was pleased to show off something she did know. "It's always colder in the mountains because they're so high up."

"I knew that," Larry mumbled.

"If there's snow, maybe I can learn to ski!" Amy said, eyes sparkling.

"Who cares about skiing?" Larry shrugged.

Larry was a klutz at skiing. Amy, on the other hand,

was good at almost every sport she tried.

I can't wait to get on a ski slope for the first time, Amy thought. Standing up on top of a steep slope would be …

Amy stopped suddenly, remembering something. She remembered that she was afraid of heights.

Standing on top of a steep slope would be … terrifying!

"You're right, Larry. Who cares about skiing?" Amy said.

Larry looked at her with surprise, then shrugged. "When are we leaving, Dad?" he asked. "I've got baseball tryouts this week."

"I know. I scheduled the trip during your school's spring vacation," Mr. Buckley said. "We won't be leaving until next weekend. Don't worry, you won't miss the tryouts."

Amy wanted to groan when she heard that. She wished Larry would miss the tryouts. Larry was as bad at baseball as he was at other sports. He probably wouldn't make the team. And if Amy made the girls' softball team, he'd be furious!

Amy sighed. It wasn't easy having an older brother who teased you all the time, but it probably wasn't easy for Larry to have a younger sister who was better at sports than he was, either.

She decided to change the subject.

"I can't wait to tell the other kids in the Explorers Club," she said.

Larry rolled his eyes. "You and your dumb club."

"Larry," Mr. Buckley said, "don't call your sister's club 'dumb'."

"But clubs are for babies," Larry said.

Amy glared at him. "The Explorers Club isn't for babies. It's for explorers who are brave and ready for adventure. You're just jealous because you're not in the club."

Larry frowned. Then he quickly switched to a big, fake smile. "I'm sorry, Amy. I didn't mean it."

"That's better," said Mr. Buckley.

But Amy looked at her brother suspiciously. Larry only acted that nice when he wanted something.

"Uh, Dad?" Larry said.

"Here it comes," Amy muttered.

"Can't I stay home instead?" Larry asked in a wheedling voice. "I'd rather practice with the team than ski on some mountain. I could stay at Brad's house."

Mr. Buckley shook his head firmly. "No, Larry. We're all going. Believe me, you'll have a good time. There's lots to do in the Alps besides ski."

"I bet there are lots of amazing things to explore in a place like the Alps," Amy said. "I just wish the rest of the club could come."

"I wish Brad could come," Larry said gloomily.

Mr. and Mrs. Buckley looked at each other and grinned.

"You just might get your wishes," Mrs. Buckley said.

*   *   *

"I can't wait to tell Curtis, Kevin, and Izzy!" That was the first thing Amy thought when she woke up the next morning.

Amy hadn't called her friends yet because she wanted everyone in the club to be together when they heard the news. She rushed through her chores, and soon was wheeling her three-speed out of the garage.

"Hey, where're you going?" Larry yelled from the open front door.

Amy braked. "I'm going to get the rest of the club."

"Oh. I thought you were going somewhere *interesting*," Larry said. He sounded sarcastic, but Amy thought he looked lonely standing there.

Being in a family that traveled a lot had helped Amy make friends. She had started the Explorers Club with other kids who also traveled. But Larry had a harder time making friends. Being away during vacations didn't seem to help. Amy suddenly felt sorry for her brother.

"Do you want to come, Larry?" Amy asked, even though she knew the other kids wouldn't like it. "You can be in the club, too."

"Well ... " Larry hesitated. Then they heard Mrs. Buckley's voice calling from inside the house.

"Larry! Brad's on the phone for you."

Brad was one of Larry's few friends. Amy thought Brad was a big bully, but Larry thought Brad was wonderful. Larry turned and ran back into the house.

Amy shrugged and took off down the street. She braked to a stop in front of a big blue house and yelled up toward one of the second-story windows.

"Yo! Curtis!"

Mrs. Wilson poked her head out of a window on the first floor.

"Amy Buckley! Now, I know your parents didn't teach you to yell like that," Curtis's mom scolded, but with a smile. "How about coming to the front door and knocking like a human being?"

On the second floor, Curtis opened his window. "Yo, Amy!" he yelled. Downstairs, Mrs. Wilson threw up her hands in defeat and retreated.

Curtis's curly brown hair was cut in a fade. His dark brown eyes blinked down at Amy through his glasses. Amy knew he'd probably been squirreled up in his room all morning, reading a book.

"Meet me at Kevin's house. We're going to the field," Amy called.

The field was an empty lot a few blocks from their houses. Sometimes the Explorers Club held its meetings there.

Curtis nodded. Amy took off from the curb and pedaled furiously down the block.

The next stop was the Medina house. Seven-year-old Isabelle Medina was sitting on the front lawn poking at a bug with a blade of grass.

"Hi, Izzy," Amy said. Nobody called Izzy "Isabelle" except her mom.

"Hi, Amy," Izzy said absentmindedly. "Guess how many legs an ant has."

"Six. Listen, I'm calling a special meeting of the Explorers Club. I've got some really important news. Go get Kevin."

"Oh, boy!" Izzy took off toward the backyard.

While Amy was waiting, Curtis pedaled up. Finally, Kevin and Izzy appeared, each wheeling a bike. The two looked almost like twins, with sandy hair sticking out from under their helmets and identical light-brown eyes. But Izzy had glasses and was much smaller than her brother. Kevin was eleven, like Curtis and Amy.

"Race you!" Amy shouted. The four of them flew

10

down the street on their bikes.

"Not fair, you guys," Izzy wailed, struggling to keep up on her one-speed.

Amy was the first to reach the field; she always was. Curtis and Kevin ground to a stop behind her. Izzy puffed her way up a minute later.

They dragged their bikes off the road and hid them in the trees lining the field. Then they each squeezed under the chain link fence and into the field.

Amy plopped down in the grass. She told them her news.

"You're going to the Alps?" Curtis asked.

Amy nodded excitedly.

"Yes," she said, "and so are you."

Curtis's jaw dropped.

"Can I come, too?" Izzy asked. "I want to go to the Ralphs."

"The *Alps*, Izzy," Curtis corrected. "It's a mountain range. That's a bunch of mountains all grouped together."

Amy rolled her eyes. Of course Curtis knew all about the Alps, she thought. He was practically a genius. Curtis had a set of encyclopedias at home and was reading every one. He was just starting "R."

"So can I? Can I come, too?" Izzy asked.

"You always want to tag along, Izzy, even when you don't know where you're going," Kevin laughed.

"That's good," Amy said. "That means Izzy is a *real* explorer."

Amy's friends were all explorers. They all traveled places with their parents. Curtis's father was a ranger who inspected National Parks. His mother traveled to research stories for magazines. Kevin and Izzy's mom

11

worked for NOAA, the National Oceanic and Atmospheric Administration. NOAA studied the weather and oceans around the world.

"The guy who hired my dad is sending over a private jet," she said. "He's letting us bring along four other people. I get to take all of you. Larry's bringing Brad Duffle."

Everyone made a face. They all knew Brad.

"Let's not talk about him," Izzy said. "Let's talk about what we'll do in the *Ups*."

"Alps," Kevin groaned.

"Whatever."

"We can go skating and hiking," Amy suggested. "I can't wait to explore."

"We've never gone anyplace as exciting as the Alps before," Curtis said. "We'll be on mountains thousands of feet high. I've never even *seen* mountains as high as that."

"Don't remind me," Amy said.

"That's right, you're afraid of heights." Kevin looked worried. "If I were afraid of heights I wouldn't get on top of some thousand-foot-high mountain. Not in a million years."

Amy had to admit she was a little worried, too. Then she scolded herself for being a scaredy-cat. "No way am I missing out on a trip like this!" she said.

Amy saw her friends sneak looks at each other. She knew they were thinking about the times she wouldn't even look out the windows of tall buildings.

"Don't worry about me," she insisted. "I can handle it."

CHAPTER TWO

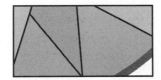

"I think I'm going to be sick!"

Amy held her stomach and moaned. The mountain-top she stood on seemed to tilt. She couldn't believe that a week ago she had said she could handle this.

I can't handle this, she thought. No way!

Just ten minutes ago, Amy had been fine, even though the small train she had been riding with her friends and family had been chugging its way to the top of a small Swiss mountain. But she had been in trouble ever since they stepped out of the train.

"There are mountains everywhere!" Curtis had gasped when they left the train. He pulled on his hat and gloves and ran across to a large viewing platform. The other kids followed Curtis. Amy's parents wandered

off to take some photos.

Even Izzy was impressed. She leaned on the low stone wall and pointed. "The mountains are all jagged, like a dragon's teeth," she said.

Amy took one quick look and felt fear sweep over her in a wave. "They look like they're ready to gobble us up," she said, forgetting that Larry and Brad were behind her.

Larry looked at Amy. A smile spread across his face. "Oh, right. You don't like mountains," he said.

Uh-oh, Amy thought. She didn't like that smile. Larry had been acting mean all week, ever since he found out he hadn't made the baseball team. And he was always worse when he was with Brad.

"What's the matter, shrimp?" Brad sneered. "Scared of heights?"

Brad Duffle had small brown eyes and stringy, dirty-blond hair. He was bigger than the school quarterback and the tallest kid in Larry's class.

Larry started to laugh.

"Ha, ha," Amy said. "You should laugh. At least I'm not afraid of snakes or water."

Larry stopped snickering. He glanced at Brad to see if he'd heard, then stalked away. Brad quickly followed.

"What do they know? I bet they've never seen mountains this big, either," Izzy muttered.

"Yeah. These mountains are gigantic," Kevin said. "They don't look real."

"They're even bigger than I thought they would be," Curtis said.

"Can you all stop talking about how big they are?" Amy practically exploded. "Just thinking about it makes me feel like I'm on a rollercoaster without a seatbelt."

"Sorry," Curtis said. "But they are amazing. Take a look. You'll see."

Amy finally looked up. Row after row of mountains unfolded around her. She could see grass growing at their bases and snow covering their tops. The ones farthest away looked like grey-blue ghosts. Amy looked down, and the view was even worse. Two blue lakes sparkled in the sun a long way down.

That's when Amy felt the world tilt.

"Don't look down!" Curtis cried when he saw her start to sway.

"I won't look at all." Amy squeezed her eyes shut. "I'm not going to open my eyes until I'm at the bottom of this stupid mountain."

"Come on, Amy, you have to open your eyes some time," Kevin encouraged her.

Amy shook her head so hard her curly red hair danced in the chilly breeze. "No way. If I open my eyes I'll see that I'm standing way up on some big rock—"

"Mountain," Curtis interrupted.

"—surrounded by lots of other big rocks so high they've got snow on their tops—"

"*Peaks.* Snow is on their peaks," Curtis said.

"—and then," Amy continued, "I'll see that waaaaay down there next to those two lakes is a nice flat place—"

"It's called a plain," said Curtis.

"—which is where I want to be RIGHT NOW!" Amy finished. "Mr. Know-it-all," she added. She opened one eye to glare at Curtis, even though she knew he couldn't help himself. He loved facts.

"At least I got you to open your eyes," Curtis pointed

out.

"One of them, anyway," Izzy giggled.

"Don't laugh," Amy said, opening her other eye. "I hate being afraid of heights."

Amy's parents joined them.

"Isn't this a fantastic view?" Mr. Buckley said.

"No," Amy muttered under her breath.

"You can even see the town where we'll be staying for the next few days. It's called Murren." Mr. Buckley pointed toward one of the mountains.

Amy groaned. He was pointing to a spot even higher than where they were now!

Mrs. Buckley put on a bright smile. "It won't be as bad as you think, Amy. You made it up here and survived, didn't you?"

Amy's parents wandered off to take one last photo. "I can't believe it," Amy complained. "They read some book about fears and now they think if I climb a few mountains, I'll stop being afraid of heights. How can my own parents be so cruel?"

"Aw, you're just chicken!"

Amy turned around.

"Get lost, Brad," she snapped.

"Buckbuckbuuuuck. Buckbuuuuck," Brad clucked.

"I'll show you," Amy said fiercely. "I'll bet you by the end of this trip I'm less afraid of heights than you are!"

"Oh, yeah?" Brad challenged.

"Yeah! Winner decides the prize."

"You're on," said Brad.

*   *   *

Despite her brave words, Amy was overjoyed when

she finally reached the bottom of the mountain.

"A train will be leaving for Murren in an hour," said Mrs. Buckley. They had arrived late the night before, so they had stayed in a town called Interlaken instead of going all the way to Murren.

"Can we explore until the train comes?" Amy asked.

"All right, but don't go too far. Meet us back at the hotel in half an hour. Your dad and I need to check out."

Amy led her friends down an empty street behind the train station. Even Larry and Brad tagged along. The street dead-ended in a patch of spongy grass by one of the lakes Amy had seen from the mountain.

Ice had formed near the edge of the lake, but had broken up in the middle where the breeze tossed the water into small, choppy waves.

"Let's slide around on the frozen part," Izzy suggested.

"I don't think we can. That ice looks pretty thin," Amy said.

"See? Like I said, you're just a chicken," Brad said. "Hey, Larry, why don't you test it?"

Larry looked at the ice and the cold blue water lapping its edges. "I don't know ... "

Brad elbowed Larry and smirked. "Go on. You're not afraid of a little water, are you?"

"Leave him alone, Brad," Amy said.

"Yeah. You do it if you're so brave," Izzy said.

"Nobody asked you," Brad snapped. "Larry wants to do it. Right, Larry?"

Larry looked like he wanted to run away. Amy was sorry she'd said anything about Larry's fear of water. She knew Brad wouldn't leave Larry alone until someone tested the ice.

"Oh, I'll do it!" Amy walked over and stepped carefully onto the ice. She took a few steps. The ice creaked under her feet.

"The ice is too thin," she called. "It would never hold you, Larry."

Amy looked at her brother's furious face and realized she'd made a big mistake. Larry obviously thought she'd done it to make him look bad.

"I'll see for myself," Larry said. Amy looked on anxiously while her brother slid a few feet onto the ice. The ice held, but the creaking got louder.

"It's okay," Larry told Brad in a relieved voice.

Brad stepped onto the ice.

"No!" Amy yelled. But it was too late. One of Brad's big feet punched a hole right through the weakened ice.

There was a terrible groaning sound. Cracks spread out crazily from the hole in every direction. Before Brad, Larry, and Amy could leap to the shore, their weight sank the floe into the water and took the three of them with it!

CHAPTER THREE

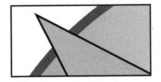

"Help me!" Larry screamed.

"No, help *me!*" Brad splashed wildly in the freezing water. "I can't swim!"

Amy just stared at them in disgust.

"You don't have to swim," she yelled. "Just stand up." She started wading through the icy water.

On the bank, Curtis, Kevin, and Izzy had burst into laughter.

"It's only three feet deep!" Curtis howled.

Brad and Larry stopped splashing and let their feet find bottom. Their faces turned beet red. Both boys stood up slowly. The water only reached their waists.

"Ha, ha," Larry said glumly when he sloshed up onto the grass. "It's not funny."

"Yes, it is!" Izzy gasped between giggles.

"If you tell anybody back home about this, I'll squash you," Brad growled at Izzy. He marched up the road toward the hotel.

"This is all your fault," Larry told his sister. He ran to catch up with Brad.

"Wait until Mom and Dad hear about this," Amy said, trudging slowly in her wet clothes up the road. "They're going to be real mad."

* * *

When Amy and the others reached the hotel, Mr. Buckley turned a fierce eye on her. "Larry says that you were fooling around on the ice and fell in. He also said he and Brad had to rescue you. Is that right?"

Amy stared wide-eyed at her brother. Larry looked away guiltily.

"That's a lie!" Amy yelled. She was so mad she thought her wet clothes would sizzle. "Brad made the ice break. And they're the ones who practically drowned, not me!"

Mrs. Buckley looked at each of them closely. Then she turned to Larry and Brad.

"One more 'adventure' and you two are grounded for the rest of the trip," she said sternly. "You, too, Amy."

"But ... " Larry whined.

Mr. Buckley frowned. "No 'buts'. You heard your mother. Now find some dry clothes in your suitcases and change or we'll all miss the train."

* * *

"Next stop, Lauterbrunnen!"

The conductor smiled at Amy as he swayed up the center aisle of the swiftly moving train. Amy looked after him in amazement.

"He said that in four different languages. He must be a genius or something," Amy said. She was sitting in a window seat next to Curtis. Across the aisle sat Kevin and Izzy.

"A lot of people here speak more than one language," Curtis said. "The Alps run through places where people speak a lot of different languages – German, French, Italian, even Serbo-Croatian."

Amy looked out the window and saw that the train was slowing down. She could see a long valley ahead. Sheer rock walls towered above either side of the narrow strip of flat land.

"It's like in *Valley of the Dinosaurs*," Kevin said, mentioning one of his favorite movies. "Only with snow. And big cliffs. And pine trees instead of a swamp."

"And no dinosaurs," Curtis added laughing. "A dinosaur couldn't climb those cliffs. They're too steep. When cliffs have really steep, flat sides like that they're called 'bluffs'."

"Was that under 'C' for 'cliff' or 'B' for 'bluffs'?" Amy teased her encyclopedic friend.

"'B' for 'boring'," Brad said from behind her. He was leaning over the seat.

"You just don't like it that Curtis knows more than you," Amy said.

Brad sneered. "Oh, yeah? If he's so smart, make him tell us why there are so many mountains around here."

Curtis glared at Brad. Then he sat up straight and

pushed his glasses up his nose.

Amy grinned to herself. You asked for it, Brad, she thought.

"The hard earth we walk on is really just a thin crust, right?" Curtis began. "Underneath it is all this molten rock – the rock is so hot it's melted."

"Rock can't melt," Brad said skeptically.

"Sure it can," said Amy. "What about lava from volcanoes?"

Curtis nodded. "Parts of the earth's crust float around on the molten rock. They're called 'plates'."

"What's that got to do with mountains?" Larry snorted.

"When two of the earth's plates meet, they smash into each other real hard," Curtis said. "Sometimes they crumple up into big folds."

Amy looked out the train window at the rows of mountains in the distance. They looked like big wrinkles in the rock. "The folds are mountains!" she exclaimed.

"Right," said Curtis. "A lot of mountains together are a mountain range, like the Alps."

Brad's face disappeared from over the top of the seat.

"Big deal," they heard him mutter.

Just then the train pulled to a stop. They all got off, then they climbed into a bus.

"This will take us further down the valley to a spot right below Murren," Mrs. Buckley explained. They rode a few miles, passing meadows scattered with white flowers and a few houses. Kevin suddenly pointed out his window.

"Take a look at that!"

Amy pressed her nose against the cold glass. "A waterfall! Dad, can we stop?"

"This is where we get off," Mr. Buckley said.

Amy ran out of the bus to get a better look at the waterfall. A stream of white water turned to foam as it shot over the bluff's edge, thundering down into a churning pool. Amy stood beside the pool, feeling cool mist from the waterfall on her face.

"A rainbow!" Amy cried.

"That's from the sun shining through the mist," Curtis explained. Then he forgot to be scientific and shouted, "Wow!"

"Wouldn't it be fun to ride down that!" Izzy said.

"No way," Kevin grabbed Izzy by the shoulders. "That sign says it's 250 meters high. That's, what, over 800 feet! Even you wouldn't want to fall that far."

"Me neither." Larry looked at Amy and the familiar wicked smile spread across his face. "I sure hope the cable car doesn't fall on the way up to Murren."

"Cable car?" Amy said weakly. "What cable car?"

Brad grinned evilly. "*That* cable car." He pointed. "The one we're riding up the cliff."

Amy looked up. And up. High above, a cable car dangled on a thin wire by the side of the bluff. As Amy watched, it inched slowly past the waterfall and ascended.

"Oh, no," Amy whispered.

CHAPTER FOUR

"Ouch! Amy, cut it out!" Curtis yelped.

Amy unstuck her fingernails from his arm. "Sorry. I thought you were the railing," she said. They were sitting with the others in the cable car. Amy held her breath as the car crawled up the face of the bluff, and she almost fainted when it swung over some jagged ridges.

Brad poked Larry with his elbow. "Looks like I'm going to win that bet."

Amy was the first one off when the car entered the station.

Mr. Buckley waved at a man hurrying toward them. "That must be Mr. Widmer. You spell it W - I - D - M - E - R, but you say the 'W' like a 'V'. He's the man who hired me," Mr. Buckley said.

Amy was disappointed to see Mr. Widmer wasn't fat and wearing short pants with suspenders, like Grandfather in the movie *Heidi*. Mr. Widmer was a thin blond man wearing a brightly colored ski parka.

"*Guten Tag!*" he said. "Hello! Come, I will take you to the hotel." They set off down the street.

"We don't allow cars in Murren," Mr. Widmer told them. "We don't want to pollute our clean air. Also, it is hard to get cars up the mountain."

It was fun walking down the middle of a street. Amy began to forget the ride up.

She checked out the town as they walked. On either side of the little village were snowy fields. On her right, the field ended at a strip of pine trees. Amy knew that the bluffs and valley were hidden beyond them. On her left, a few small mountains looked tiny compared to a giant peak towering behind them.

"That's the Schilthorn," said Mr. Widmer, following Amy's glance. "It is almost 3,000 meters high."

Amy did some lightning-quick multiplying. "Wow! That's almost 10,000 feet!" She hoped no one would suggest visiting the top.

"Look, a ski lift," Larry said, pointing at the base of the mountain. "I guess Amy won't be using it," he said smugly.

Amy bit her tongue to stop herself from replying that Larry's clumsy skiing kept him confined to the bunny slopes.

They arrived at the hotel a moment later. A teenaged girl was waving from a balcony on the second floor of the pretty wooden building.

"Ah, there is my daughter, Margrit," Mr. Widmer said proudly. "She is 16. I am sure she will be happy to show you children around."

The girl leaning over the railing had thick, curly blonde hair and bright blue eyes. Amy's heart sank. Larry and Brad acted even dumber around pretty girls.

"I think I'm in love," Larry sighed.

Amy groaned inside. If Margrit acted as dopey around boys as Larry did around girls, this was going to be a long vacation.

Margrit appeared on the steps in front of them and was introduced. Then Amy's parents followed Mr. Widmer into the hotel.

"Guh … Gooiter Tal," Larry said, obviously hoping to impress Margrit by imitating Mr. Widmer's German greeting.

"Yeah. Gooiter Tal," Brad said, making his voice sound deeper than usual.

Amy perked up when she saw Margrit roll her eyes over Larry's and Brad's puppy-dog stares.

"*Gewitter Tal?*" Margrit barely hid a smile. "No, I do not think there is a thunderstorm in the valley."

Amy giggled. "*Guten Tag*," she said, remembering Mr. Widmer's exact words.

"Right. *Guten Tag*. That's what I said," Larry mumbled. He turned bright red.

Brad stepped in front of Amy. "So, Margrit, how about leaving these kiddies here and showing us around?"

Margrit thought for a moment, then said sweetly, "I have a better idea. Do you two like to ski?"

"Oh, sure, I'm an ace on skis. I ski everyday back home," Larry babbled.

Amy's jaw dropped.

"Me, too," Brad lied. "I'm just about the best skier in Maryland."

"Would you like to go skiing this afternoon?" Margrit asked.

"Sure," said Brad. "Maybe we can give you a few lessons."

"Oh, no. Since you are so good, you would not want me along. I don't ski so well." Margrit stepped to the stairs and called, "Ernst!" Then she turned back to Larry and Brad. "You will have more fun with Ernst. He is an expert like you."

Ernst bounced into the room. He was a short, round-cheeked boy about Margrit's age. Margrit spoke to him in German and Ernst grinned.

"Ja, ja," he said, grabbing Larry and Brad by their elbows.

"But ... but ... " Larry began as he and Brad were led away.

Amy grinned at Margrit.

Margrit smiled back. "Now we can have some fun," she said.

*   *   *

"Where are we going?" Amy asked. A half hour had passed since their arrival in Murren. They were headed across a snowy field toward a hill covered by a pine forest.

Margrit gestured to a boot-trampled trail that wound into the forest.

"Along the trail is a spot where you can see all of

Murren," she said and led the way.

They trudged through the snowy woods to a rocky point where they could look down at Murren. Remembering her bet with Brad, Amy forced herself to look down. Fortunately, the town wasn't far below.

"Murren looks so pretty, all covered with snow," Amy said.

"That's funny," said Curtis. "It looks like it just snowed here, but it wasn't snowing on that mountain we were on this morning."

"I know why," Kevin said, proud he could tell Curtis a new fact. Kevin had learned a little about the Alps' weather from his mom and NOAA. "Every valley and mountain around here has its own weather. It depends on how high up you are and how the wind blows around each mountain."

"That is true," Margrit agreed. "It did snow here earlier, but now it is too warm."

Amy wasn't listening. She had just heard something even more interesting.

"Listen," she said. "Do you hear bells?"

"They're probably cowbells," Curtis said. "I saw a herd of cows in the fields down on the plateau."

"The what-oh?" Izzy asked.

"*Plateau*. That big flat place in between the sides of the bluffs," Curtis said.

"There are many sheep and cows in the Alps. It is much easier to raise animals than crops on a mountain," Margrit explained.

"I bet," said Curtis. "Except for places on the plateaus, the fields would have to be laid out practically sideways. Kind of hard to use a tractor on that."

Margrit shook her head and laughed. "No, our farms are on flat terraces. They are cut into the rock and look like steps up the mountain."

From far away came another chorus of musical chimes.

"We will be able to see the cows from another spot. Follow me," Margrit said. She led the way through the pine forest.

"It seems colder in the woods," Amy observed, zipping her ski jacket right up to her chin.

"And darker," said Kevin. The trees cast deep blue shadows on the snow. He shivered.

"Hurry a bit if you're cold," Margrit suggested. She broke into a jog and disappeared around a clump of tall evergreen bushes.

Amy was about to follow when she heard a strange sound from the trail behind them. She stopped dead in her tracks. "What was that noise?"

"What noise?" Kevin instantly looked nervous.

"It sounded like this." Amy made a low growling sound deep in her throat.

"I didn't hear anything," Izzy said.

"Maybe it was just a squirrel," Kevin said hopefully.

"Listen," Amy insisted. She heard another noise. It was a loud cracking and rustling, like something large pushing its way through the bushes.

"Too big for a squirrel," Kevin gulped.

"Maybe it's one of those cows we heard before," Curtis said.

A second later, they all heard the low growling sound.

"That's one sick cow," Izzy commented.

"That was no cow," Amy said. She started backing away up the trail. "That sounded more like a bear — "

" — or a wolf." Curtis was right behind Amy.

"Or an Abominable Snowbeast," Kevin added, mentioning one of his favorite movie monsters.

Amy thought she saw a big, hunched shape moving through the shadows beneath the trees.

"Let's get out of here," she hissed. Amy took off up the path at a run. She hadn't gone far when she heard someone howl in fear. She stopped and looked back.

"I'm stuck!" Kevin's ski jacket had snagged on a jagged bush. Amy saw that he was tugging at it furiously, staring in terror at the shadowy path behind him.

Kevin yanked his jacket free just as Amy heard another loud, low roar. She saw a large shape launch itself from the shadows.

"Kevin!" Amy screamed as the beast leapt on her friend.

CHAPTER FIVE

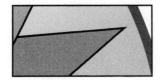

"Get off me! Stop, you're tickling!"

Kevin's yell of terror had dissolved into helpless giggles.

Amy couldn't believe her eyes. The thing that had jumped on Kevin wasn't a bear or wolf. Nor was it an Abominable Snowbeast.

"It's a dog!" Izzy said.

"What's going on? I heard someone scream." Margrit came running down the trail. When she saw the dog licking Kevin's face, she stopped.

"Wolf! What are you doing here? You're supposed to be home," she scolded. "Bad dog, Wolfie!"

Wolf let loose a low whimper. He climbed off Kevin and wandered over for a pat. Amy took off her mittens and dug her fingers into his thick red-and-white fur.

"Wolfie is a Saint Bernard," she said. She recognized the breed's big head and shoulders.

Margrit smiled. "Right. They are a popular breed here. Their fur keeps them warm, and they are good trackers. Wolfie was trained as an avalanche dog but I am afraid he failed some of his tests."

"An *avalanche* dog?" Curtis asked. "You mean one of those dogs that finds people who have been buried in the snow?"

"What's an alva ... avla ... what you just said?" Izzy asked.

"*Avalanche*," Kevin put in. "It's when a big pile of snow and ice slams down the side of a mountain. They're awesome!"

Margrit nodded. "And frightening. It takes many months to train a dog to find someone who has been buried in an avalanche. There is a school for rescue dogs in the Great St. Bernard Pass."

"I read about that," Curtis told the others. "This Saint Bernard guy built a monastery in one of those pathways through the mountains. People kept getting lost when they tried to get through the pass, so the monks trained dogs to find people."

"Wolf tracked us here all the way from the hotel by following my scent," said Margrit. "He is very good at that. It was his other tests that he failed."

"Does he carry a little barrel like in cartoons?" Izzy asked. She peeked under the dog's chin. "Yuck. There's nothing but drool down there," she reported.

Wolf put his big paws on Izzy's shoulders, making her stagger. Then he licked her face with his pink tongue.

"Eeewww! He kissed me!" Izzy pushed the dog away and wiped her mittened hand across her face.

"He likes you," Amy said.

"I like him, too. But next time, just shake paws, okay Wolf?" Izzy held out her hand and the dog put his heavy paw on it. Then he licked her face again.

"Yuck!"

*   *   *

Amy was glad when they decided to head back toward Murren. She was cold, even with her snug ski jacket and mittens.

"I bet Larry is freezing on the slopes," Amy said as they passed the ski lift. "Let's go watch him. It should be fun."

They walked to the bunny slopes to get a better look at the skiers.

"Can any of you see Larry?" Amy asked. "His jacket is black and red."

Amy and her friends scanned the top of the gentle bunny slope. Larry was nowhere in sight. Amy glanced over at the much steeper advanced slope. The clean snow glowed in the bluish-pink afternoon light. Skiers zigzagged down, leaving snakelike trails in the snow.

"It's getting late," Margrit noted. "Soon they will shut down the lift."

Someone skied up to them and braked suddenly in a big whoosh of snow. It was Ernst. A second later, Brad skied up beside him. Despite Brad's earlier bragging, his whoosh wasn't so good. He landed on his backside.

"Where's Larry?" Amy asked Brad as he struggled to

his feet.

"Up there," Brad said. He pointed up the mountain with his ski pole. He wasn't pointing at the bunny slope. Amy squinted and saw a black-and-red figure just beginning to ski down the advanced slope. He was one of the last ones left.

"Larry shouldn't be up there!" Amy cried. "He's not good enough."

Ernst shrugged. "I tried to keep him off."

"Yeah," Brad said. "We couldn't stop him."

"You did not try," Ernst reminded him. "You told him only babies stayed on the bunny slope."

Amy glared at Brad. "Larry'd better be okay."

She moved closer to the bottom of the hill and watched as the tiny red and black figure started down. Larry zigzagged shakily a few feet, then fell over. The last skiers passed him on either side. Larry got up, skied a bit farther, then fell over again.

Amy hid her face behind her mittens. "How could he be so bad at sports?"

She peeked again and saw Larry fall over a third time.

"Look at it this way," Kevin said encouragingly. "If he keeps falling down, at least he won't be going fast enough to hurt himself."

"We could be here all night," Curtis said.

This time, though, Larry made it three-quarters of the way down the hill before falling over.

Amy watched her brother stagger back to his feet and start hunting for his ski poles. A moment later he started gliding smoothly down the slope.

"Wow, look! Larry's skiing backwards," Izzy said. She turned to Amy. "He must be getting better if he's doing tricks like that."

Amy gasped. "He's not doing that on purpose," she cried.

Larry was sliding backwards down the slope, faster and faster. He tried looking over his shoulder. That only made him veer off course.

Amy started to run up the slope. "We've got to help him!" she called over her shoulder. "He's lost control and he's backing into those trees!"

CHAPTER SIX

"Hit the deck!" Amy shrieked at her brother.

Larry was sliding clumsily toward the woods bordering the ski slope. Amy tried running faster, but going uphill in the snow was almost impossible.

"Fall down!" Amy screamed. She knew that her brother's only hope was to fall into the snow before he reached the thick wall of trees.

This time, Larry heard her. He launched himself sideways.

"Yeeooowwwwww!" Larry's shout echoed down the mountain. He cartwheeled over the snow, missing a pine tree by inches. His skis flew off and slid down the hill. Snow tumbled down in his wake in a crystalline heap.

Amy came to a stop. Her friends struggled up the

slippery slope beside her.

"Where is he?" Amy cried as the snow settled. Larry had disappeared in a cluster of drifts.

Suddenly, a furry red-and-white shape bounded up the hill past Amy.

"Follow right behind," Margrit ordered. "It is easier to walk in Wolf's pawprints. He will find Larry."

Wolf seemed to swim through the drifts, using his big paws like flippers.

Amy leaped from pawprint to pawprint. At the spot where Larry had disappeared, she arrived just in time to hear, "Get away from me. Yuck! Get lost!"

Amy dropped on her knees in the snow and looked down at her brother, who lay half-buried in the snow.

"Larry! Are you okay?"

"Of course I'm not okay!" Larry looked angrily up at his sister. Snow clung to his hair and eyelashes. "I'm being licked to death by some wild animal. Now quit laughing and get me out of here!"

*   *   *

Larry was still sulking the next morning.

"I'm telling you, it was the skis. They don't make them the same here," Larry grumbled through a mouthful of granola cereal and milk.

The six kids were having breakfast with Margrit in the hotel dining room. Margrit had happily offered to play tour guide that day, so Amy's parents had gone off with Mr. Widmer to inspect the ski lift.

Amy felt sorry for Larry. She knew how he must feel. First he hadn't made the cut on the baseball team.

Then, even worse, he wiped out on a ski slope in front of a girl he wanted to impress. Amy only hoped he wouldn't take his anger and embarrassment out on her.

Larry looked at Amy. "Hey, little sister, did you hear where we're going today?" he said.

"No. Where?" Amy asked. She braced herself.

Margrit didn't know abut Amy's fear. "I thought you all might enjoy a trip up the Eiger," she said. "It is one of the tallest mountains in this region."

Brad grinned. "Looks like I'm going to win that bet."

Amy definitely would not enjoy a trip like that. She was about to say so when she noticed Brad's toothy grin grow wider.

"Sounds great!" Amy said, mustering a smile.

*   *   *

"I'm getting really tired of train rides up mountains," Amy complained to Kevin a few hours later.

"Well, we're not going up this one, we're going through it," Kevin pointed out.

Sure enough, the train tracks led right into the side of the mountain ahead.

"We are inside the Eiger now. It is a long way over the mountains. Sometimes it is faster and easier to go through them instead," Margrit said.

While they were still in the dark stone tunnel, the train began to slow down.

"Why are we stopping?" Amy asked.

Margrit smiled mysteriously. "Get out and see."

The kids followed the crowds piling off the train.

"Hey, look! It's a window," Izzy cried in disbelief. She

ran ahead of the others to a big glass wall set into the rock. Amy followed more slowly. She had a feeling she wouldn't like the view.

"Cool!" said Kevin, peering down through the glass. "It's like you're hanging right over the side." He glanced at Amy. "I wouldn't look down if I were you."

Izzy was fearless. "We're even higher than the trees," she said, craning her neck to look straight down.

"You mean we're above the timberline," Curtis said.

"No, I mean we're higher than the trees," Izzy insisted. Curtis rolled his eyes.

Margrit stared down the steep, iron-gray rock. "That mountainside has killed many people," she said sadly.

Amy looked at her with wide eyes. "How?"

"People die every year trying to ski down the north face of the Eiger. Skiers and climbers often die in the Alps when they take foolish chances."

Amy shot a glance at Larry, who was pretending not to hear.

They got back on the train. It chugged out of the tunnel back into the sunshine and climbed further up the side of the mountain. It finally pulled to a stop at a station that sat on a shelf-like ledge of snow-covered rock.

"This is the highest railway station in the world," Margrit said when they stepped onto the platform.

"I believe it," Amy said, gasping for air.

"I feel kind of funny," Izzy said. "Like I've just blown up about a hundred balloons."

Margrit laughed breathlessly. "The air is much thinner this high up. It takes time for your lungs to get used to the altitude. But now we will go even higher. An elevator will take us to the Sphynx Terrace. You will get the

44

best view from there."

Amy moaned. A few minutes later she found herself on a ledge 36 stories above the railway station, looking out over a huge stretch of gleaming snowfields.

"Brrrr. It's freezing up here," Amy said. The air was like ice in her lungs. Her friends' noses were already cherry red.

"It's cold, but I'm glad Margrit told us to bring sunglasses," Curtis said. "The sun on the snow is really bright."

Nearby, three enormous mountains loomed like giants, their sharp ridges poking through blankets of blinding white snow. The valleys below were so far away they blurred in the distance. Amy gulped, but was surprised to find she didn't feel sick. Well, not too sick anyway. Maybe she was getting used to heights.

"What's the name of that mountain?" Izzy asked. "That really big one over there, covered with clouds?"

"That is the Jungfrau," said Margrit. "It is called that because some people say it looks like a young woman, a 'jung Frau' in German."

Izzy squinted at the mountain. "It just looks like a big rock to me."

"Look how smooth the snow is on that big patch over there," Kevin said, pointing. "It's like a big river of ice."

"I bet that's a glacier," Curtis said.

"Glaciers are only in Alaska," Larry said.

Curtis shook his head. "Glaciers are in lots of cold places. They helped shape the Alps. See all the grooves in the mountains? That's erosion from glaciers moving down the sides and wearing away the rock."

"A glacier can't move. It's frozen solid," Brad said.

"Glaciers *are* frozen. But they move around on a stream of water. A little bit of the ice melts underneath, because it's rubbing against the rock," Curtis explained.

"How can that make it melt?" Izzy asked.

"Rub your hands together," Curtis told her. "Like this." He stripped off his gloves and demonstrated.

"I know what happens," Izzy said, keeping her mittens firmly on her fingers. "Your hands get warm. Anybody knows that."

"That's friction," Curtis said. "The glacier rubs against the rock and it gets warm underneath. Warm enough to melt the ice a little. Then the glacier moves."

"He thinks he's soooo smart," Brad said.

"He is," Margrit said. She smiled warmly at Curtis. "There is even a marker by one of the glaciers so you can measure how far it moves."

"What's so interesting about a big blob of ice, anyway?" Larry grumbled. Amy could see that Larry and Brad were jealous about Margrit's attention to Curtis.

"Lots," said Curtis, who obviously hadn't noticed he was making the older boys steam. "Some hikers recently found a body in a glacier in the Alps. The body was all dried up like a raisin. I saw a show about it on television."

"Big deal," Larry scoffed.

"It is. This body was from prehistoric times. Scientists took some of its skin and put it in chemicals until it fell apart. Then they were able to tell how old it was," said Curtis. "The body was five thousand years old."

"How do you know so much?" Margrit asked Curtis admiringly. "Are you in the same grade as Larry and

46

Brad?"

Amy winced. Her brother was turning red again. In another minute he was going to erupt. But before that could happen, they heard a low rumbling in the distance.

Amy saw movement over by the glacier. "Over there!" she shouted. Everyone on the terrace ran to the railing for a look.

As Amy and her friends watched in amazement, one of the snowy slopes above the glacier seemed to collapse. It thundered down in a huge explosion of icy powder.

"It's an avalanche," Amy gasped as another huge chunk of snow roared down the mountain.

Margrit nodded solemnly, "The white death."

CHAPTER SEVEN

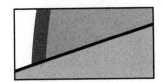

"Do you have avalanches in Murren?" Amy asked
Margrit.

The next morning they were all still talking about
what they'd seen the day before. Amy's parents hadn't
come down for breakfast yet so the kids were once
again eating by themselves.

Margrit nodded. "Avalanches sometimes fall near the
base of the Schilthorn. I would not be surprised if there
were avalanches today, because it snowed last night
and is supposed to be warmer today."

"Why does that make it more dangerous?" Curtis
asked curiously.

"The top layer of snow melts and does not grip the
slope," Margrit explained.

"You wouldn't catch me near that mountain today," Amy said with a shiver.

"Or any other day," Larry laughed. Amy made a face at him.

"In some towns, they build fences along the mountains to catch snow when it falls. Here, my father and some other townspeople sometimes plant explosives to make the snow fall," Margrit said.

"You mean your dad makes avalanches by using bombs?" Izzy was delighted.

"Only very little bombs," Margrit laughed.

"I get it. Instead of waiting for the snow to fall by itself, you make it fall," Curtis said. "That's smart. You control the avalanche. You can do it when there's no one around to get hurt."

"What should we do today, if we can't go hiking?" Amy asked. She was secretly glad to have an excuse not to go near the mountains, even if it meant losing her bet.

"I thought you might like to go skating at the sports center," said Margrit.

"That's for little kids," Brad snorted. "I want to go skiing again."

"I do not think that is a very good idea," Margrit said. "Besides, after what Larry did, the instructors said you two must stay on the bunny slope."

Amy's heart sank. That was the wrong thing to say.

"Well, I'm not going skating with a bunch of babies!" Larry said, his voice rising. "You'll see!"

Larry raced out of the dining room, followed by Brad.

Amy was worried. She knew Larry. Now he'd feel like he had to prove himself to Margrit. It was just a matter of time before he got into trouble.

Larry reappeared a few minutes later carrying his backpack. Brad held a piece of paper.

Larry put on a smug smile. "We're going hiking," he said.

"Oh, no, you're not," Amy said.

"Oh, yes, we are," Brad mimicked. He shoved the piece of paper under Amy's nose. "We've got a trail map and we're going."

Margrit grabbed the map and looked at it closely.

"What if an avalanche gets you?" Kevin said in a worried voice.

"We'll be careful," Larry said. But Amy could tell he was a little scared at the thought.

"Being careful is not enough," Margrit said with a serious look on her face. "The trail you have marked here is for experts. You are not experienced enough to hike it alone."

Amy groaned. That was definitely the wrong thing to say.

Larry flushed. "We're not as dumb as you seem to think," he said. "We're going!"

"Mom and Dad won't let you. Here they come now," Amy said with relief.

Mr. and Mrs. Buckley sat down at the table. They were in the middle of a conversation of their own.

"I'd love to go, honey, but I don't want to leave the children alone again," Mrs. Buckley was saying to her husband. "Margrit's probably tired of being a tour guide."

"Go where?" Amy asked.

"I'd like to take a look at a new ski lift in the next

town over," Mr. Buckley said. "I won't be back until late this afternoon. I was telling your mother that she'd love the skiing there. Some of the slopes are for real experts."

"Please go," Margrit urged. "I like being a tour guide. I was going to take everyone to the sports center today, anyway." She looked sternly at Larry and Brad.

Mrs. Buckley caught the glance. "What about you boys?"

"We'll keep ourselves busy," Larry said with an angelic smile.

Amy could see that her parents were suspicious.

"We're not leaving until everyone promises—no more adventures," Mr. Buckley said.

Larry sighed. "All right, I promise." The others promised, too.

Mrs. Buckley hesitated, then smiled. "Okay, I'll go. But you listen to Margrit and Mr. Widmer while we're gone."

"And Margrit says you cannot go hiking," Margrit said to Larry as soon as his parents left. "Put your bag back in your room. You are coming with us."

Amy thought Larry would argue. She was as surprised as the others when he smiled and said, "Sure, sure. Whatever you say."

*   *   *

"My feet are freezing," Izzy said. They had all spent the last few hours ice skating on the rink at the sports complex. The huge center had an indoor pool and tennis courts, as well as the big rink.

"You should have worn more than one pair of socks," Kevin said.

Kevin, Curtis, and Amy were taking a break from practicing some fast-paced ice hockey moves. They joined Margrit and Izzy, who were resting.

"It's not really that cold out, Izzy," said Amy.

"It seems cold to me," said Izzy. She turned to Curtis. "Rub my feet to make some friction."

"Ew, yuck!" Curtis said. "I wouldn't touch your stinky feet with a hockey stick."

"We should head back to the hotel," Margrit suggested. "It is lunchtime anyway."

"Okay," Izzy said. She bent down and began untying her ice skates. In seconds the laces were in impossible knots.

"Where are Larry and Brad?" Kevin asked as he helped Izzy with her laces.

Amy shrugged. "I don't know. I haven't seen them for a while. Maybe they went back already."

They turned in their skates and headed for the car-free street.

"I feel like I'm floating," Izzy sang as she waltzed up the road.

Curtis laughed. "She's right. After wearing skates, even my snowboots feel like Air Jordans." He took off down the street at a gallop.

They raced back to the hotel. Amy won, as usual.

Larry and Brad weren't in the dining room or the arcade.

"Let's check their room," Amy suggested. She led everyone up the stairs to the room Brad and Larry were sharing. A knock brought no answer. Amy tried the door. It was unlocked.

Inside, they found two unmade beds and mounds of dirty clothes.

"Look at this mess," Amy said. "I guess the maids haven't been here yet."

Izzy held up a sock and sniffed. "Pewww!"

"Put that down," Kevin said. "You're being gross."

Izzy shook her head. She sat down on the bed and unlaced her boots. "I'm going to wear them. They're stinky, but they'll keep my feet warm," she announced.

"Put on a pair of your own socks," Kevin told her. She ignored him.

Amy was also poking around the clothes on the floor. Suddenly, her eyes grew wide.

"Larry's backpack is missing," she announced. She looked up at Margrit with a worried expression. "I think they went on that hike after all!"

Margrit hurried to the balcony. It looked out over the imposing Schilthorn. "I hope they have not done anything foolish. It is the warmest part of the day."

Amy joined her on the balcony. She remembered what Margrit had said before. A warm thaw after a heavy snow was dangerous. It could lead to ...

" ... the white death," Amy whispered.

A low rumble penetrated the glass. At first, Amy thought she had imagined it. But the rumble was real.

"It's an avalanche!" Amy looked at Margrit in terror. "Can you tell where it is? Is it anywhere near that trail Larry was talking about?"

Margrit slowly turned to Amy and nodded.

CHAPTER EIGHT

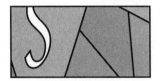

"We've got to do something!" Amy wailed.

They rushed out of the room, found Margrit's father, and told him that Larry and Brad might be victims of the avalanche. Mr. Widmer made some calls and soon the area outside the hotel was filled with townspeople from Murren. The Explorers Club joined the search party.

"What are those long sticks they're carrying?" Izzy asked.

"Those are probes," Margrit said. "The rescue team uses them to look for people under the snow. They stick them into big drifts to see if anyone is buried there."

Buried. Amy shivered. That was her brother they were talking about. "Let's go," she said anxiously.

At that moment a woman came around the hotel. She held two more dogs on leashes. One was a Saint Bernard, the other was a big German shepherd.

"Here comes Anni. She has the best-trained dogs in Murren," said Margrit, who was also bringing Wolf along. Margrit shrugged a coil of sturdy rope over her shoulder. "Do not worry, Amy. We will find your brother."

But Amy was scared. It might already be too late to save Larry and Brad if they had been caught in the avalanche.

In a matter of minutes, the team was ready. They traveled across snowy fields to the rocky base of the Schilthorn. Signs marked an area where several trails began.

"This one," said Mr. Widmer. He started hiking up one of the tracks. Margrit had told him about the trail marked on Larry's map.

Amy could see that the trail wound up and up the mountain before it disappeared around some sheer rock walls. She and her friends took off after Mr. Widmer.

"Don't worry, we'll find Larry," they kept reassuring Amy.

"This path is so steep, it's more like climbing than walking," Amy said. The slippery melting snow made it even harder.

"Your brother picked one of the most difficult trails," Margrit commented breathlessly.

"He was trying to impress you," Amy said. Margrit frowned.

"I'm sure he didn't bargain for something this hard," Curtis said.

Soon, even athletic Amy was panting with the effort. She tried not to notice the sheer drop on one side of the path.

After a half hour another rumble echoed down the mountain. This one sounded very close. Mr. Widmer motioned everyone to stop.

"It is the prime time of day for more avalanches," he said to Margrit. "I was foolish to place the children in danger by letting them come. You must take them back to the hotel."

"No!" Amy pleaded. "I want to help find my brother."

Mr. Widmer shook his head firmly. "The team must concentrate on finding the boys, not looking after more children. Margrit, promise you will take them back."

"At least take Wolf," Margrit said.

Her father shook his head. "Wolf is a good puppy, but he is not a true avalanche dog. No, you take him back with you. He is just a distraction to the other animals."

Margrit nodded, but she looked angry at the insult to her beloved pet.

Amy watched the rescue team walk away around a bend. She stomped back down the path. Her friends followed in silence. They had been walking for almost fifteen minutes when they passed a small yellow boulder half-buried in the melting snow.

"Why is that rock painted yellow?" Izzy asked.

"Different-colored rocks mark different trails," Margrit told her. "That yellow one is much easier than the trail we were on."

Amy stopped in her tracks. She stared at the yellow rock. "Was this easier trail marked on that map?" she asked Margrit.

Margrit nodded. "But it was not the one Larry was talking about. He had marked the other trail with a pen."

"Listen, I have an idea," Amy said. "Larry was trying to show off. That's why he said he was going on that tough trail. But he really doesn't like hiking. I bet he took this easy one instead."

"Maybe we should get my father," Margrit said.

Amy shook her head. "I could be wrong. Let them check the other trail. We'll explore this one." She marched past the yellow rock.

"But I promised my father we'd go back to the hotel," Margrit said.

"And I promised my parents no more adventures," Amy said. "But finding Larry is more important." She walked off down the other trail, sure the others would follow. They did.

The new trail wasn't as steep as the one they had just climbed. For a while it wound through tall green spruce trees. The snow was covered with dry red needles.

"It smells like Christmas," Izzy said.

When the trees thinned they could see other mountains cast long shadows in the distance.

"We must hurry," Margrit said. "We do not want to get caught in the mountains after dark."

The trail passed through a flat area next to a sheer, snow-covered rock wall. Then it wound back into the woods.

Amy kept expecting to see Larry around each bend. But as long minutes dragged by, she started to give up hope.

"Maybe I was wrong," Amy said sadly. And then things got worse. Up ahead the trail split in two.

"Which way did they go from here?" Margrit asked.

Amy groaned. "There are footprints on both paths."

"Let's use Wolf! He can track people," Curtis said.

Margrit shook her head. "Wolf can sniff out someone buried in the snow, but he can't track a specific person unless we give him a scent. He can follow me because he remembers what I smell like, but he does not know Larry or Brad."

Izzy started jumping up and down. "Wait! I've got socks!"

Kevin rolled his eyes. "We all have socks, Iz."

"No, no!" Izzy said impatiently. "I have Larry's socks, the ones I took to keep my feet warm. I never took them off." She started unlacing one of her boots. Amy was dancing with impatience by the time Kevin helped Izzy untangle the knot.

Amy grabbed the sock and shoved it under Wolf's nose. "Here, Wolfie, smell this."

Wolf sniffed the sock over and over.

Amy watched, biting her lip anxiously. After a minute Wolf's ears pricked up. He shook his furry head, then raced up the path to the left. Amy took off after the dog.

Wolf led them through a grove of spruce. The trees protected the snow from the sun so the ground was still covered in a thick white blanket.

"It's hard to walk," Kevin said. Sometimes they crunched through the stiff top layer of snow and had to pull their booted feet back out. It was harder for Margrit, who was taller and weighed more. She crunched through at almost every step.

After a while, only two sets of footprints marked the snow ahead of them.

"Those must have been made by Larry and Brad," Amy said in excitement.

Wolf paused. He started whining softly.

"Why has he stopped?" Amy said. "I don't see Larry."

"Wait!" Margrit said sharply. "Wolf has found a crevasse."

Amy stopped at the sound of alarm in Margrit's voice. "A 'crevasse'? What's that?"

"It's a crack in the ice," Curtis supplied.

"A crevasse can be very wide," Margrit said. "But sometimes it is only a few feet wide and the top can become clogged with snow. Then it would be completely hidden."

"You mean, someone could walk over it ... and fall through?" Kevin asked in a small voice. Margrit nodded grimly.

Amy leaned forward. Sure enough, she saw a hole in the snow ahead. Suppose Larry and Brad had walked over the snow, unaware of the crevasse hidden beneath? The hole was about four feet wide. Amy thought two boys walking side by side might make a hole like that.

"Larry!" Amy screamed.

"Amy? Is that you?" a familiar voice replied. It sounded far away. "Oh, man, am I glad you found us."

Amy sagged with relief at the sound of Larry's voice–until she heard his next words.

"We're on a ledge, but the edge keeps crumbling. I don't know how long it'll hold!"

"This crack's a mile deep at least!" Brad's voice

added in a wail. "You've got to get us out of here."

Amy tried to picture a drop a mile long. Just the thought of it made her feel faint. But her brother was down there! She took a step toward the hole.

Margrit reached out and grabbed Amy. "No, you can't. We don't know where the real edge is under that snow. You might fall in, too."

"But we have to see where they are and whether we can rescue them!" Amy cried. She shook off Margrit's hand, took a deep breath and walked toward the hole.

The snow dissolved under her feet.

CHAPTER NINE

Amy teetered for a second on the edge. She drew in a frightened breath and scrambled backward. Her feet just found the edge of the ice.

The others ran over to join her.

"That was close!" Kevin cried.

Amy nodded. She could hardly speak. Looking down into the crevasse was worse than the view from any mountain. The sides went almost straight down. The thought that she had almost fallen in made her feel sick. But the fact that Larry had fallen in made her shake off her fear.

"Are you alright?" Amy asked her brother.

"Oh, yeah, we're just fine," Larry said sarcastically. "We're sitting on a crumbly ledge ten feet down in some crack, but we're fine."

It made Amy dizzy just looking at him. The ledge he was standing on looked more like a clump of frozen snow than rock. And beyond that there was nothing but a deep drop into the stony heart of the mountain.

"We f-fell." Brad was stuttering from cold and fear. "We must have w-wandered off the trail. Next thing we knew there was nothing under us."

"Lucky for you there was a ledge," Curtis commented.

"No kidding," Larry said. "Now use those smarts everybody's always talking about and get us out of here."

Larry was acting brave, but Amy could see that he was scared. She was just glad her brother was afraid of water and not heights.

"Do you think we can get the rescue team here before it gets dark?" Curtis asked.

"No way are you leaving us here!" Larry said. "This ledge is pretty shaky."

Brad let out a wail. "If you leave us here much l-longer we're going to freeze to d-death. I p-put my sweater and gloves in Larry's b-backpack. We lost it when we fell."

"Try friction!" Izzy yelled down to them.

"We have to get them up before it gets dark," Margrit said.

"We can use your rope," Amy suggested.

Margrit nodded. She shrugged the coil of rope off her shoulder.

"Let's tie one end to a tree," Curtis suggested. "Then they can climb up."

"Does anybody know how to tie a good knot?" Kevin asked. "I only know the one you use on shoes."

"That wouldn't be strong enough," Margrit said.

"Maybe if Izzy tried to tie the knot, she'd make one of her famous tangles. Those are almost impossible to get loose," said Kevin.

Amy snatched the rope impatiently. "Am I the only Scout around here?" she said.

She marched to the nearest tree and looped one end around its thick trunk. Then she expertly tied a double-eight knot. Amy tossed the other end down to her brother.

"Climb up," she called down to him.

The Explorers Club and Margrit crowded close to the edge to watch Larry and Brad. It took only a few minutes to see that they needed a new plan. Neither boy could get more than a few inches up the rope.

"It's not easy climbing this thing, you know," Larry panted. "It's slippery and my hands are frozen."

"We'll just have to pull them up," Amy said.

Margrit looked down at the teenagers below, then at the younger kids beside her. "Even with all of us pulling, I'm not sure we're strong enough. Both of them look pretty heavy," she said.

"We'll have to try," Amy said. She pulled up the rope and tied another knot, leaving a big loop at the end. She tossed it back into the crevasse.

"Larry, put that loop around you, under your arms. Try climbing as we pull, then you can help us with Brad," she said.

When Larry was ready, Amy pulled up the slack. She walked away from the edge and grabbed onto the tough yellow nylon. Behind her, the other kids did the same.

"This is just like tug of war," Izzy said.

They gave a huge tug.

"Hey! Be careful up there!" Larry yelled. "You almost cut me in half."

No one replied. They were all straining to pull Larry up. The icy snow was slippery underfoot. They moved back a few steps. Then Curtis's boots slid out from under him. He fell, letting go of the rope. Without his weight, the rope began snaking backward over the edge.

Amy felt herself, Kevin, Izzy, and Margrit start sliding toward the crevasse. Wolf started barking loudly.

"Let go!" Curtis yelled. "You'll get dragged in!"

The others let go of the rope just a second before Amy reached the edge.

"Sorry, Amy," Curtis gasped.

"That's okay," Amy said. She looked over the edge.

"Why did you let go? I could have fallen all the way down," Larry sputtered from the ledge.

"No, you couldn't," Amy said. "We left the other end of the rope tied to a tree." But she noticed that more of the ledge had crumbled into the crevasse from Larry's sudden landing.

"Try again!" Brad wailed. "I gotta get off this ledge or I'm gonna d-die!"

"And don't drop me this time," Larry begged.

"Come on," Amy told her friends. "We can do it!"

The others nodded, but Amy could see they didn't really believe it. They were tired from the first try.

Amy tried to think of something to get them psyched up for another attempt. Suddenly, Amy stuck out her arms and put both fists on top of each other. Kevin, Izzy,

and Curtis quickly joined her and stacked their fists on top of hers. Then they all broke away, shouting, "Goooooooooo Explorers!"

"Wooooooooooof!" Wolf joined in.

"What is that?" Margrit said, staring at them.

"That's our club handshake," Amy said. "We're the Explorers Club and we can do anything. Right, you guys?"

"Right!" Curtis, Kevin, and Izzy said. They each grabbed a handful of rope.

Amy dug her heels into the snow. "Let's go."

They pulled and pulled, straining and sliding.

"My arms are falling off!" Izzy moaned.

"Just ... hang ... on ... one ... more ... minute," Amy muttered behind clenched teeth. Her muscles were screaming, too.

There was a sharp tug on the rope.

Amy whipped around; her heart thudded in fear. Had Larry slipped through the rope?

Larry was lying on the trail. "I made it! I'm up!"

"We did it!" Amy yelled. The rescuers jumped up and down and cheered.

Just then they heard a weak cry from the ledge. It was Brad.

"Hey you g-guys! Don't f-forget about me!"

*   *   *

Amy felt like dancing with joy when they finally pulled Brad out of the crevasse. They were all safe again! But if she had expected thanks, she was wrong.

"Let's go, I'm freezing," was all Brad said before walking quickly back the way they had come.

Amy shrugged. She guessed Brad was embarrassed that they'd seen him when he was so scared, which was stupid. It *had* been scary.

Larry acted only a little better than Brad. "Thanks," was all he said before taking off after his friend.

"Next time let's leave them on the ledge," Izzy muttered.

The rescuers untied the rope and had to run to catch up with Larry and Brad. They had left the woods and reached the wide flat space next to the rock wall. The setting sun made the sheet of snow on the wall sparkle with red sparks. Amy didn't notice the scenery. She had been thinking.

"You know, Brad," Amy said. "I went up the mountain looking for you guys and then I stood right on the edge of that crevasse. I figure that means I win our bet."

Brad kept walking, his arms wrapped around himself for warmth.

"No way! You were still scared, I could tell." Brad looked at Larry. "Right, Buddy?"

Brad hardly ever called Larry "Buddy." Amy knew whose side Larry would be on now.

Larry avoided his sister's angry eyes. "I'm glad you rescued us and all, Amy. But Brad's right. You haven't won yet."

"What?" Amy spluttered.

She stopped in the trail and looked around. A remark like that deserved an icy snowball down the back. She stomped a few feet away to where a big snow boulder lay half-buried. It looked firmer than the melting snow around her. She knocked off a piece and packed it into a ball. She tossed it up and down in her mittened hand.

"Perfect," she said softly to herself. The others had gone ahead of her up the path. Larry was pretty far away, but Amy was an ace pitcher.

"Look out, Larry," Amy muttered. She had cocked one arm for the throw when she heard a loud groaning. It was immediately followed by a sound that cracked the air like a gunshot.

Amy saw Margrit and the others stop up ahead.

"Avalanche!" Margrit screamed. "Amy, run!"

Amy looked around wildly. On the slope above the trail a long crack had opened in the snow. A huge slab of wet snow began to slide down below the crack. It was right above Amy. She started to run.

The slab of snow moved slowly at first, then gathered speed. It came thundering down the slope with a roar so loud it hurt Amy's ears. Amy could see that her friends had already reached a spot safely past the slab's path. If only she could reach them in time!

"Run, Amy! You can make it!" she heard Larry screaming.

Amy was the fastest runner in her class in Harkin Heights. But she had been many yards behind the others when the avalanche began. She felt a wall of snow slam into her with the force of a football tackle.

Amy was covered by a deep wave of ice and snow.

CHAPTER TEN

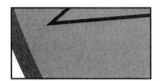

The roar of the avalanche pounded in Amy's ears as she was catapulted forward. Her heart jumped into her throat and her mind was a jumble.

The massive slab of snow tumbled Amy over and over. She felt herself sinking deep into the snow. The wet stuff filled her eyes and mouth. Amy choked. If she didn't get out, she would suffocate.

Swim. From out of her mixed-up thoughts, one idea rang like a bell. Amy remembered the way Wolf had seemed to swim through the snow.

Amy started to dog paddle. She swept her arms in front of her and kicked. After a few seconds, Amy was sure she had stopped sinking. But she was blinded by the snow and had no idea which way was up.

Moments later, the roaring stopped and the snow seemed to settle around her. Amy "swam" harder.

She kicked and paddled. Rocks and branches that had been carried along with the avalanche scraped her hands and face. Amy's lungs felt like they were bursting. She gasped for air and choked on a mouthful of snow.

Somebody help me, Amy thought. Everything was growing black.

Something thumped her hard on the back. Then a pair of red and black gloves appeared in front of her eyes. They dug furiously at the snow in front of Amy's face.

The minute her mouth and nose were uncovered, Amy swallowed a big gulp of air. It tasted wonderful!

A cluster of arms reached down and pulled Amy from the snow. Even Brad helped. Amy took some deep breaths and shook her wet hair out of her face. Her hat was gone.

Amy smiled at her friends gratefully and suddenly knew how Larry must have felt back at the crevasse. "Thanks," was all she could say, too.

"Wolf found you," Margrit said proudly as she helped Amy to her feet. "My father was wrong. He is a true rescue dog after all."

Amy was having trouble standing on her wobbly legs. She dropped to her knees to hug Wolf and didn't even mind when he licked her.

"We have to get you back right away," Margrit said in concern. "You'll freeze in those wet clothes."

"I'm freezing, too," Brad reminded them.

Curtis lent Amy his jacket. They all hurried along the trail.

"What was it like?" Kevin asked Amy after a minute.

"It was like being buried alive." Amy shuddered. She told them about what she'd experienced. "It was the scariest thing that has ever happened to me."

"Even scarier than being on a mountain?" Larry said with a sideways glance.

"I told you, I'm not afraid of heights anymore," Amy told him, hoping it was true. After the avalanche, it didn't seem like a little thing like a mountain could scare her again. "That reminds me. I *did* win that bet!"

"Well, I'm the one that dug you out of that avalanche!" Larry retorted.

Amy stared at him in surprise.

"You did?"

"It's true," Izzy reported. "He got there just after Wolfie. He uncovered you before we even reached you."

Larry turned beet red and shrugged. "Big deal," he said to Amy. "Now you owe me one."

A wide smile spread across Amy's face. "No way. But you and Brad can forget about the bet. This makes us even."

Larry smiled. "Okay, brat. Even-steven."

"Yeah, okay," said Brad.

Amy figured that watching her get buried in an avalanche must have been almost as scary as actually being buried in one. That was the only thing that could explain why Larry and Brad were being so nice.

Amy knew it wouldn't last. Pretty soon, both boys would be picking on the Explorers Club again. She figured she would get in the first shot.

"I have another bet for you," Amy said to Larry and Brad.

"Oh, yeah?" said Larry.

"I bet I know something that will scare you."

Larry looked at her. "What?"

"Mom and Dad."

Larry's eyes widened. "They'll ground me for life!"

"My father will be angry with me, also," Margrit said glumly. "We were all supposed to go straight back to the hotel. When he hears that Amy has been in an avalanche ... ." She shrugged. "Not even the fact that we saved the boys will make him forget I disobeyed him."

"Woof," Wolf barked sadly in agreement.

"Wait until my parents hear about the avalanche," Amy said.

"Uh-oh," Kevin said. "Remember, we promised: no more adventures."

Amy looked at her friends. They were covered with snow and dirt from their two rescues. She started to giggle.

"No more adventures?" she gasped. "That's impossible. We're the Explorers Club!"

WHERE ARE THE ALPS?

The Alps run through parts of France, Switzerland, Italy, Austria, Germany, and what was formerly Yugoslavia. The tallest peak in the Alps, Mont Blanc, is in France and is almost 16,000 feet. Murren, where the Explorers Club stayed, is in the Oberland section of the Alps, in south central Switzerland.

 The black area on the map is Switzerland.

 The gray lines show the Alps.

If you have enjoyed this book, you may like to read The Explorers Club's first adventure: *Storm at the Shore*, also written by Betsy Loredo, and illustrated by Michael Moran

GLOSSARY

Alps: A mountain range that runs through South Central Europe.

Bluff: A steep hill or mountainside with a wide, flat face.

Cliff: A section of land that is worn away by wind, water, or the movement of glaciers.

Crevasse: (pronounced "kri-VAS") A deep crack in a glacier, earth, or rock.

Crust: The outer shell of the earth. It is a cool layer of rock that is more than 40 miles thick in some places.

Erosion: The wearing away of something–like rock or earth–by wind, water, or the movement of glaciers.

Fold: A bend in rock caused by the movement of the earth's crust. Some mountains are called "fold mountains" because they were formed this way.

Glacier: A huge slab of ice that acts like a very slow-moving river. It can move down a slope or valley, or spread out over a flat section of land.

Ledge: A shelf of rock that sticks out from the side of a rock wall.

Molten rock: Rock that is so hot it has melted and acts like a liquid.

Plate: A section of the earth's crust.

Plateau: (pronounced "pla-TOE") A flat section of land that ends at the edge of a cliff or bluff.

Slope: Ground that slants up or down.

Terrace: A narrow plain with a steep drop on one side and a wall on the other.

Tree line: The place where trees stop appearing on a mountain. Above the tree line it is too cold and there is not enough soil for trees to root. This is also called the "timberline."

Valley: A flat section of land, usually between hills or mountains. Sometimes valleys are dried up riverbeds.

MAKING A MOUNTAIN

Curtis told everyone how the movement of the earth's crust helps to create mountains. Try this experiment in mountain-making.

You will need:

• **Modeling clay, in two or three different colors**
• **Waxed paper**
• **Two big pieces of plain, smooth paper**

1. Make thick sheets out of the clay by rolling it out over the waxed paper.

2. Lay the sheets of clay on top of each other in layers. Alternate the colors so you have three obvious layers.

3. Spread out the two sheets of paper so their sides overlap by at least an inch.

4. Peel your clay stack off the waxed paper and lay it over the two sheets of plain paper. The clay represents the earth's crust. The different colors are different layers of rock. The two sheets of paper are the molten rock that the crust rests on.

5. Now, push two opposite sides of the clay toward one another. The section in the middle will rise up into folds. Look at the clay from the side and see how the different layers have been squeezed up into an upside-down-U-shape. When plates on the earth's crust meet, there is so much force it causes folds, even in rock. These are mountains, which form on either side of the place the plates meet.